Cactus Soup

BY ERIC A. KIMMEL
PICTURES BY PHIL HULING

two lions

two lions

Amazon Publishing, Attn: Amazon Children's Publishing, P.O. Box 400818, Las Vegas, NV 89140
www.amazon.com/amazonchildrenspublishing

Library of Congress Cataloging-in-Publication Data
Kimmel, Eric A.
Cactus soup / by Eric A. Kimmel ; illustrated by Phil Huling.— 1st ed.
p. cm.
Summary: During the Mexican Revolution, when a troop of hungry soldiers
comes to a town where all the food has been hidden, they charm the
townspeople into helping make a soup from water and a cactus thorn.
ISBN 978-0-7614-5832-6 (paperback)
[1. Folklore—France.] I. Huling, Phil, ill. II. Title.
PZ8.1.K567Cac 2004
398.2'0944'02—dc21
2003009110

The illustrations are rendered in watercolor and inks on watercolor paper.

Editor: Margery Cuyler
Printed in China

NE DAY

a troop of soldiers came riding
toward the town of San Miguel.

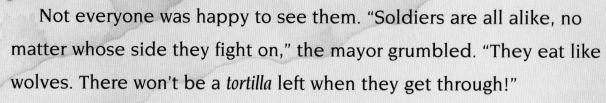

Not everyone was happy to see them. "Soldiers are all alike, no matter whose side they fight on," the mayor grumbled. "They eat like wolves. There won't be a *tortilla* left when they get through!"

"What should we do?" the people asked.

"We'll do what we always do," said the mayor. "We'll hide our food and tell the soldiers we have nothing to give them. They'll leave when they see they aren't going to be fed."

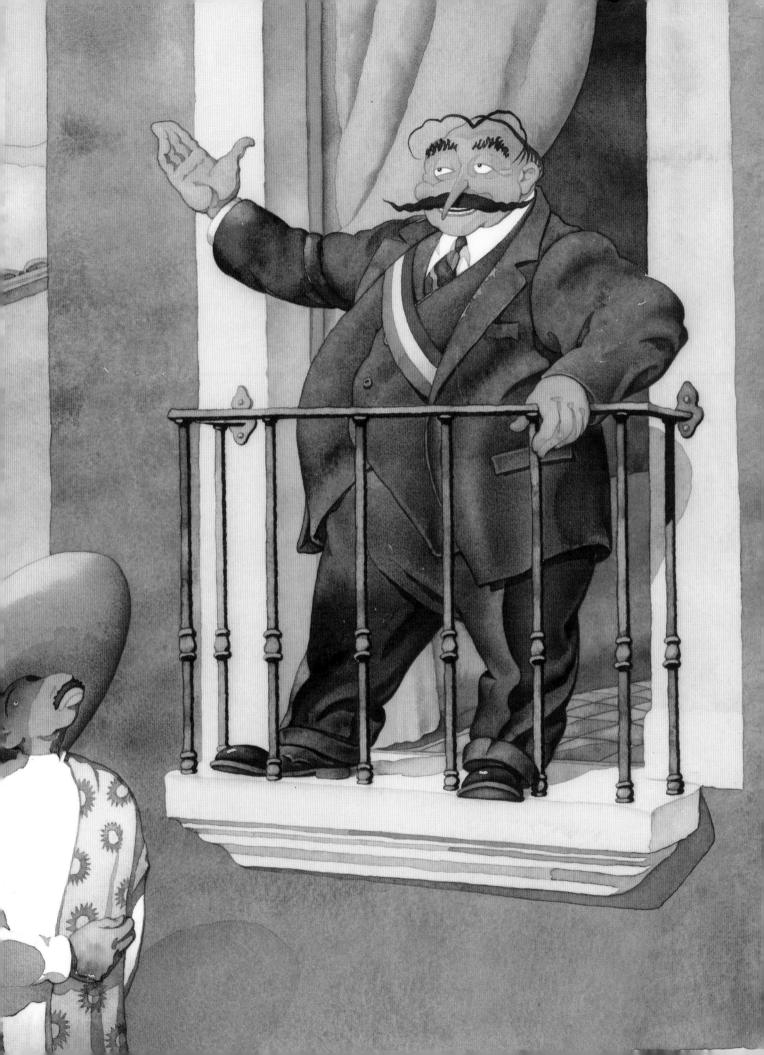

Everyone in San Miguel went to work. They buried sacks of beans and cornmeal in their gardens and lowered baskets of *tortillas* and *tamales* into the old stone well. Some hid chickens under their beds and ducks and geese in the bathtubs. Several carried pigs up to the rooftops while their neighbors herded cows and sheep into the cellars. The children hung strings of *chile* peppers high in the trees where no one would see them.

Once that was done, the townspeople put on torn, dirty clothes, smeared mud on their faces, and tried their best to look like poor, hungry people.

The soldiers came riding into town on prancing horses. They wore wide *sombreros*, with leather *bandoleras* slung across their chests. The captain saluted the mayor and townspeople.

"*Señor Alcalde*, my *compañeros* and I have been riding all day. We're tired and hungry. Can you spare some beans and *tortillas*? We would be so grateful."

The mayor frowned. "I am sorry, *Señor Capitán*. As you see, our town is very poor. Other soldiers came by the other day. They ate the few beans and *tortillas* we had. Now we have nothing. There isn't even enough for the little ones."

The parents nudged their children, who began crying bitterly, just as they had practiced.

"What a pity," the captain said. "Did you hear that, *amigos*? There's nothing to eat in this town. It looks like we're going to have to make cactus soup."

"Oh no!" the soldiers cried. "Not cactus soup *again*!"

"Stop complaining," the captain said. "Cactus soup is better than no soup at all."

The children stopped crying. Everyone in the plaza leaned forward to listen as the mayor asked, "What is cactus soup?"

"You'll see," said the captain. "I'll make enough for my soldiers and everyone in town. However, I'm going to need help. Can you bring me a kettle of water, a stirring spoon, plenty of firewood, and one cactus thorn? We have lots of people to feed, so bring the biggest thorn you can find."

The mayor ordered everyone to help. A kettle of water was soon boiling in the plaza. Cactus grew everywhere in town. The children had no trouble finding a huge thorn as long and as sharp as a needle.

"This thorn will make plenty of soup!" the captain exclaimed. He dropped it into the kettle and began stirring.

"How can anyone make soup from a cactus thorn?" asked the priest.

"Watch carefully. Perhaps we'll learn something," whispered the mayor.

The people of San Miguel looked on as the captain stirred. And stirred. And stirred. He lifted the spoon, blew on it, let it cool, had a taste. "Not bad," he declared, as he continued stirring. "I always find that a pinch or two of salt improves the flavor. But never mind. I know how poor you are. Why ask for what you don't have?"

"We have salt," said the mayor. "We're not as poor as that."

"And pepper, too," the town clerk added. "Does cactus soup taste good with *chiles*?"

"Cactus soup is outstanding with *chiles*!" the soldiers exclaimed.

People tripped over themselves running home to fetch salt. The children climbed trees to bring down strings of *chile* peppers. The captain stirred the salt and *chiles* into the soup. He took another taste.

"It's getting better," he declared. "Too bad you don't have onions. Cactus soup always tastes better with onions. But why ask for what you don't have?"

"I know where I can find some onions," said the priest.

"What about garlic?" asked the sacristan.

"Garlic makes excellent soup," the captain answered. The priest and the sacristan ran to the church. They came back a few minutes later with a sack of onions and several heads of garlic. The captain chopped up the vegetables and dropped them into the kettle.

"Smell that soup!" he exclaimed, as he continued stirring.

The people of San Miguel sniffed the air. "Soup that smells this good must taste wonderful!" cried the members of the town council.

"If only we had some beans. And carrots. And tomatoes. And perhaps even a fat stewing hen. Then our soup would really have flavor," said the captain. "But it's fine the way it is. Why ask for what you don't have?"

The townspeople winked at each other. "Come with us," they told the soldiers. They returned in a few minutes, carrying sacks of beans, bunches of carrots, baskets of tomatoes, and several fat stewing hens.

"The hens were old," said the mayor. "They wouldn't have lived much longer."

"The tomatoes were spoiled," said the barber.

"The beans were rotten," said the school teacher.

"The carrots were moldy," said the shoemaker.

"Never mind," said the captain, as he stirred and stirred the ingredients into the thick, rich soup. "That's the best part of cactus soup. Whatever you add makes it taste good. Mmm! I think it's ready now. Who wants to try some?"

"Me!" Everyone lined up in the plaza, bowls in hand. The captain ladled out the soup.

"This is the best soup I ever ate!" said the mayor.

"I never tasted anything like it!" said his wife.

"And to think it was made from a cactus thorn!" exclaimed the priest.

"Not bad!" said the captain. "However, I think cactus soup always tastes better when you have something to go with it."

"Such as?" all the people asked.

"*Tortillas*! *Tamales*! Sweet potatoes! A roasting pig!" cried the soldiers.

"That would make for a real *fiesta*," the captain said. "And some music, too, for dancing later on. However, I know how poor you are. Why ask for what you don't have?"

"Wait here," the mayor told the soldiers. He whispered orders to everyone in town. They all ran home—and came back carrying *tortillas*, *tamales*, *chorizo*, *camotes*, and several fat roasting pigs.

What a feast they had! As the night wore on, soldiers and towns-people ate until they couldn't hold another bite. Then they brought out accordions and guitars for singing and dancing.

The *fiesta* lasted until dawn. Nobody in town could remember anything like it.

The soldiers rode away in the morning. The people of San Miguel gathered in the plaza to wave good-bye.

"What will we do if more soldiers come?" they asked the mayor, when the last soldier disappeared from sight.

"Let them come, the more the better," the mayor replied. "Feeding soldiers is no trouble. We can feed a whole army and have a *fiesta* every night, as long as we remember how to make . . .

Cactus Soup!

Pancho Villa   *Emiliano Zapata*

Author's Note

The story of "Stone Soup" or "Nail Soup" appears in cultures around the world. I chose to set this version in the time of the Mexican Revolution, which lasted from 1910 to 1922. Under leaders such as Pancho Villa and Emiliano Zapata, the common people of Mexico struggled to take back political and economic power from the wealthy classes and foreign business interests that controlled most of the country.